Toby

Based on
The Railway Series
by the
Rev. W. Awdry

Illustrations by
**Robin Davies and
Jerry Smith**

EGMONT

EGMONT

We bring stories to life

First published in Great Britain in 2016
by Egmont UK Limited
The Yellow Building, 1 Nicholas Road, London W11 4AN

Thomas the Tank Engine & Friends™

CREATED BY BRITT ALLCROFT

HiT entertainment

ISBN 978 1 4052 7986 4
62424/1
Printed in Italy

Written by Emily Stead. Designed by Claire Yeo.
Series designed by Martin Aggett.

FSC
MIX
Paper
FSC® C018306

This story is about Toby the Tram Engine. Toby felt sad because some people said he was too old-fashioned. Then one day someone special came to his rescue . . .

Toby was a tram engine, with cowcatchers, side plates and a coach called Henrietta. Toby always felt happy when he was busy working on his little line near a holiday town.

Toby and Henrietta worked hard, taking trucks from the farms to the Main Line. But they didn't have many passengers.

Henrietta wished she had more passengers. "The buses are always full, even though they often have accidents," she grumbled. "We never have accidents, but nobody wants to travel with us."

Sometimes the people on the buses laughed at Toby and called him **old-fashioned**. This made Toby feel sad.

One day, a car stopped nearby and two children jumped out.

"Wow! Look at this engine!" said the little boy.

"That's a tram engine," explained a stout gentleman. "It's a special kind of steam train."

"Can we have a ride in it?" asked the little girl. "Please!"

When everyone had climbed into Henrietta, the Guard blew his whistle and Toby set off.

"Hip, hip, hurray!" Henrietta cheered as they steamed away.

Everyone enjoyed the ride. "Thank you, Toby. We'll come back soon," they promised.

"Peep! Peep!" whistled Toby. "We would like that."

As the weeks passed, there were only a few trucks for Toby to pull. And there weren't **any** passengers!

"It's our last day, Toby," his Driver said one morning. "The Manager says we must close tomorrow."

At the end of the day, Toby puffed back to his Shed. He didn't feel like a Useful Engine at all.

But the next morning, Toby had a big surprise. His Driver held up a letter. It was from the stout gentleman.

"That gentleman was The Fat Controller," his Driver told Toby. "He needs an extra engine on his Railway and he wants it to be **you**!"

Toby beamed from buffer to buffer! What exciting news!

Toby and Henrietta set off the same day, feeling very excited. The Fat Controller came to meet them at Tidmouth Sheds.

"I hope you'll work hard and be a Useful Engine, just like Thomas," The Fat Controller smiled.

"I will, Sir!" **peeped** Toby.

Thomas showed Toby what to do and they soon became good friends.

It didn't take Toby long before he was a Really Useful Engine.

Next to Thomas' Branch Line was a little cottage. Mrs Kyndley lived there. She was poorly and had to stay in bed, but she loved to wave to the engines as they puffed past.

They always whistled a friendly, **"Peep! Peep!"** to cheer her up.

One rainy day, Thomas was puffing down the track with Toby following behind.

When they reached Mrs Kyndley's house, a big red cloth was waving from the window.

"Something's wrong!" said Thomas. He steamed to a stop, just before a bend in the track.

Thomas' Driver and Fireman hurried towards the cottage. But when they reached the bend, they saw why Mrs Kyndley had tried to stop the train.

"A landslide!" said the Driver. "Mrs Kyndley was trying to warn us!"

She had seen the blocked tunnel, and waved her dressing gown out of the window like a danger flag! Clever Mrs Kyndley!

The next day, Toby and Thomas brought a new dressing gown, grapes and some coal to say thank you to Mrs Kyndley.

Mrs Kyndley was delighted. Toby blew his whistle happily, **"Peep! Peep!"**

He was proud to be a tram engine in Sodor's Steam Team.

More about Toby

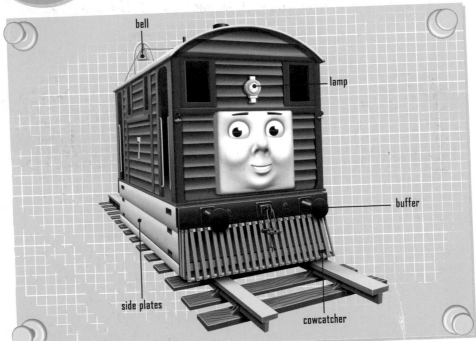

bell

lamp

buffer

side plates

cowcatcher

Toby's challenge to you

Look back through the pages of this book
and see if you can spot:

letter

plant pot

blue wheel

kite

red cloth

THE *THOMAS* ENGINE ADVENTURES

From Thomas to Harold the Helicopter, there is an Engine Adventure to thrill every Thomas fan.

 Thomas

 James

 Percy

 Harold

 Spencer

 Henry

 Toby

 Gordon

 Cranky

 Flynn

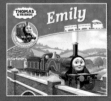 Emily

 Hiro